SHUTTER ISLAND

DENNIS LEHANE
CHRISTIAN DE METTER

SHUTTER ISLAND
Based on the Novel by Dennis Lehane
Graphic Novel Adaptation by Christian de Metter

English Adaptation - Bryce P. Coleman
Layout and Lettering - Lucas Rivera
Production Artist - Michael Paolilli
Cover Design - Al-Insan Lashley

Editor - Bryce P. Coleman
Print Production Manager - Lucas Rivera
Managing Editor - Vy Nguyen
Senior Designer - Louis Csontos
Director of Sales and Manufacturing - Allyson De Simone
Associate Publisher - Marco F. Pavia
President and C.O.O. - John Parker
C.E.O. and Chief Creative Officer - Stu Levy

A  Manga

TOKYOPOP and  are trademarks or registered trademarks of TOKYOPOP Inc.

TOKYOPOP Inc.
5900 Wilshire Blvd. Suite 2000
Los Angeles, CA 90036

E-mail: info@TOKYOPOP.com
Come visit us online at www.TOKYOPOP.com

WILLIAM MORROW
An Imprint of HarperCollinsPublishers
www.harpercollins.com

ISBN: 978-0-0619-6857-0

First TOKYOPOP printing: October 2009
10 9 8 7 6 5 4 3 2 1
Printed in the USA

SHUTTER ISLAND

BASED ON THE NOVEL BY
DENNIS LEHANE

GRAPHIC NOVEL ADAPTATION BY
CHRISTIAN DE METTER

TOKYOPOP®

HAMBURG // LONDON // LOS ANGELES // TOKYO

WILLIAM MORROW
An Imprint of HarperCollinsPublishers
www.harpercollins.com

Thanks, Angelique and Hugo.

To my father and brother.

For Hugo.

YOU OKAY?

FINE. I MAY BE A FISHERMAN'S SON, BUT I CAN'T STAND BOATS.

THEY SAY IT'S GONNA BE BAD.

WHAT IS?

THE STORM. WEATHERMEN SAY IT'S A BIG ONE.

YOU WERE IN THE WAR TOO, RIGHT? HOW OFTEN WERE THEY RIGHT ABOUT THE WEATHER?

TRUE ENOUGH.

YOU BEEN A MARSHAL LONG?

FOUR YEARS. HIT BOSTON A WEEK AGO. I'M FROM SEATTLE. MY GIRLFRIEND'S JAPANESE.

WELL, SHE WAS BORN HERE, BUT GREW UP IN A CAMP. STILL A LOT OF TENSION OUT IN OREGON, YOU KNOW, AND PEOPLE DIDN'T LIKE SEEING US TOGETHER, SO THEY MOVED ME.

SMOKE?

WHAT'D I DO WITH MINE? HAD THEM WHEN I BOARDED...

TAKE IT. MY TREAT.

YOU MARRIED?

I WAS.

SHE'S DEAD.

CHRIST, I'M AN IDIOT. I HEARD ABOUT THAT. DON'T KNOW HOW I FORGOT.

DON'T SWEAT IT.

THERE WAS A FIRE IN OUR BUILDING. I WAS WORKING. FOUR PEOPLE DIED. THE SMOKE GOT HER, CHUCK, NOT THE FLAMES.

DRANK A LOT BACK THEN. AFTER THAT, I STOPPED.

SO...HEARD MUCH ABOUT THIS PLACE?

NOT MUCH. A MENTAL HOSPITAL, THAT'S ALL I KNOW.

FOR THE CRIMINALLY INSANE.

RIGHT. ELSE WHY WOULD WE BE ON THIS OL' TUB?

THEN AGAIN, YOU DON'T LOOK A HUNDRED PERCENT STABLE YOURSELF.

FROM WHAT I UNDERSTAND, THEY SPECIALIZE IN RADICAL APPROACHES. WHAT EXACTLY DO WE KNOW ABOUT THE WOMAN WHO'S GONE MISSING?

ONLY THAT SHE ESCAPED LAST NIGHT.

FIGURE THEY'LL FILL US IN ON US THE REST.

HELLO, GENTLEMEN. I'M DEPUTY WARDEN MCPHERSON.

GENTLEMEN, YOU'LL BE ACCORDED ALL THE HELP WE CAN GIVE, BUT DURING YOUR STAY, YOU WILL OBEY PROTOCOL.

UNMONITORED CONTACT WITH THE PATIENTS OF THIS INSTITUTION IS STRICTLY FORBIDDEN.

WARD A--THE BUILDING BEHIND ME TO THE RIGHT, IS THE MALE WARD, AND WARD B--TO MY LEFT, FOR FEMALES. WARD C--IN WHAT WAS ONCE FORT WALTON, IS BEYOND THE BLUFFS, BEHIND THE STAFF QUARTERS.

ACCESS IS FORBIDDEN WITHOUT WRITTEN CONSENT AND THE PHYSICAL PRESENCE OF BOTH THE WARDEN AND DR. CAWLEY. UNDERSTOOD?

GOOD. NOW, BY THE AUTHORITY VESTED IN ME, YOU ARE HEREBY REQUESTED TO SURRENDER YOUR FIREARMS.

MR. MCPHERSON... WE'RE DULY APPOINTED FEDERAL MARSHALS.

WE ARE REQUIRED BY FEDERAL ORDER TO CARRY OUR FIREARMS AT ALL TIMES.

EXECUTIVE ORDER 391 OF THE FEDERAL CODE OF PENITENTIARIES AND INSTITUTIONS FOR THE CRIMINALLY INSANE STATES THAT THE OFFICER'S REQUIREMENT TO BEAR ARMS IS SUPERSEDED BY ORDER OF HIS SUPERIOR, OR THAT OF PERSONS ENTRUSTED WITH THE CARE AND PROTECTION OF PENAL OR MENTAL HEALTH FACILITIES.

FINE. BUT WE'D LIKE OUR OBJECTIONS NOTED FOR THE RECORD.

THEY'LL BE RETURNED WHEN YOU LEAVE.

YOU'LL MEET THE WARDEN LATER. WHAT SAY WE GO SEE DR. CAWLEY?

WHAT'S THAT TOWER?

AN OLD LIGHTHOUSE. HASN'T BEEN USED SINCE THE 1800S. IT'S A TREATMENT FACILITY NOW.

FOR PATIENTS?

SEWAGE.

Y'KNOW, CAWLEY'S A LEGEND IN HIS FIELD. SCOTLAND YARD, THE OSS, MI:5 — THEY'VE ALL CONSULTED HIM MANY TIMES.

WHY WOULD THE OSS NEED A SHRINK?

WAR WORK.

RIGHT, BUT WHAT KIND?

TOC TOC

THE TOP SECRET KIND, I SUPPOSE.

DR. CAWLEY, THESE ARE MARSHALS *DANIELS* AND *AULE*.

THANK YOU, MR. MCPHERSON.

MARSHAL TEDDY DANIELS.

GLAD YOU COULD COME SO QUICKLY, MARSHAL DANIELS.

MARSHAL AU...?

AULE. CHUCK.

CHUCK... I ASSUME YOUR FIRST NAME IS CHARLES.

CHARLES SUITS YOU, BUT I'M NOT SO SURE ABOUT YOUR SURNAME.

I DIDN'T GET TO CHOOSE.

PLEASE -- HAVE A SEAT.

AND IS TEDDY SHORT FOR THEODORE?

EDWARD.

HMM... MY WIFE'S NAME IS MARGARET, BUT EVERYONE CALLS HER PEGGY.

I'VE NEVER UNDERSTOOD WHY.

WELL. HAS THE SENATOR EXPLAINED THE SITUATION?

WE DON'T KNOW ANY SENATOR. THE STATE FIELD OFFICE GAVE US THIS CASE. ALL WE KNOW IS A FEMALE INMATE IS MISSING.

A PATIENT... YES. *RACHEL SOLANDO*. LAST NIGHT BETWEEN TEN AND MIDNIGHT.

IS SHE CONSIDERED DANGEROUS?

ALL OUR PATIENTS WERE PUT HERE DUE TO THEIR *VIOLENT PROCLIVITIES.* SHE'S A WAR WIDOW. DROWNED HER THREE CHILDREN IN THE LAKE BEHIND HER HOUSE, THEN PULLED THEM OUT AND SAT THEM AROUND THE DINNER TABLE.

A NEIGHBOR STOPPED BY, AND SHE ASKED HIM IN TO BREAKFAST. HE'S THE ONE WHO CALLED THE POLICE.

OH, MY GOD...

IS IT HER BEAUTY, OR HER MADNESS YOU'RE REACTING TO?

BOTH.

I'M GUESSING YOU'VE ALREADY SEARCHED THE GROUNDS?

WE SCOURED THE ISLAND AND ALL ITS BUILDINGS THIS MORNING. NOT A TRACE.

WE HAVE NO IDEA HOW SHE EVEN GOT OUT OF HER ROOM. IT'S AS IF SHE EVAPORATED STRAIGHT THROUGH THE WALLS. BUT I SUGGEST YOU GO AND TAKE A LOOK FOR YOURSELVES.

AS YOU CAN SEE, THERE WOULD'VE BEEN NO PLACE FOR HER TO HIDE.

YOU SAID ALL PERSONNEL ARE REQUIRED TO SIGN THE KEYS TO THESE ROOMS IN AND OUT. I'D LIKE TO SEE THAT LOG.

CERTAINLY.

AND THE PERSONNEL FILES, TOO.

DOCTORS, ORDERLIES, AND GUARDS.

WHAT FOR?

A WOMAN DISAPPEARS FROM A LOCKED ROOM, AND THERE'S NO TRACE OF HER ON A TINY ISLAND? SORRY, BUT I HAVE TO AT LEAST CONSIDER SHE HAD SOME HELP.

I'LL CHECK WITH WARDEN ST--

IT WASN'T A REQUEST. WE'RE HERE ON GOVERNMENT ORDERS TO LOCATE A DANGEROUS PRISONER. IF YOU DON'T COOPERATE, YOU COULD FACE CHARGES...

OF OBSTRUCTING JUSTICE.

I'LL DO ALL I CAN TO HELP YOU FIND OUR... PATIENT.

HOW MANY PAIRS OF SHOES ARE PATIENTS ALLOWED?

TWO.

SO SHE LEFT BAREFOOT?

HERE, LOOK AT THIS. IT WAS BEHIND THE DRESSER.

WE HOPE YOU CAN MAKE SOMETHING OF IT.

The Law of 4

I am 47
They were 80

+ You are 3

We are 4
But
Who is 67?

DOESN'T MEAN A THING.

THERE ARE THREE OF US HERE.

NOW HOW COULD SHE HAVE KNOWN THAT?

RACHEL IS MOST INGENIOUS WITH HER GAMES.

HER HALLUCINATIONS ALLOW HER TO BELIEVE HER CHILDREN ARE STILL ALIVE.

BUT THEY REST ON A VERY DELICATE FOUNDATION. IN ORDER TO MAINTAIN IT, RACHEL WOVE AN ELABORATE AND COMPLETELY FICTITIOUS NARRATIVE THREAD INTO HER LIFE.

SHE NEVER ACKNOWLEDGED SHE WAS IN A MENTAL HOSPITAL.

SHE BELIEVED SHE WAS AT HOME, AND WE WERE ALL MAILMEN, MILKMEN, OR DELIVERYMEN STOPPING BY.

THE TRUTH NEVER GOT THROUGH? SHE MUST'VE HAD SOME IDEA THAT SHE WAS IN A HOSPITAL.

THAT'S THE BEAUTY OF SCHIZOPHRENIC'S PARANOID STRUCTURE. IF YOU ALONE KNOW THE TRUTH, THEN EVERYONE ELSE MUST BE LYING, AND IF EVERYONE IS LYING--

THEN ANYTHING THEY SAY IS THE TRUTH MUST BE A LIE.

THAT STAIRWAY'S THE ONLY EXIT? ANY WAY UP TO THE ROOF?

THERE'S A FIRE ESCAPE WITH A GRATE ACROSS IT, LOCKED AT ALL TIMES. WE EVEN CHECKED.

AND SOMEONE'S HERE DAY AND NIGHT?

YES. *MR. GANTON* WAS HERE LAST NIGHT.

SO RACHEL LEAVES HER LOCKED ROOM, GETS PAST AN ORDERLY, THANKS TO HER INVISIBILITY, AND REACHES...

OUR COMMON AREA. PATIENTS SPEND THEIR EVENINGS THERE. YESTERDAY THERE WAS A GROUP THERAPY SESSION. AFTER LIGHTS OUT, THE ORDERLIES ARE SUPPOSED TO CLEAN THE ROOM, BUT USUALLY THEY STAY AND PLAY CARDS.

AND LAST NIGHT?

THE GAME WAS IN FULL SWING. THE ONLY EXIT IS AT THE FAR END OF THE ROOM. SO UNLESS SHE REALLY WAS INVISIBLE...

2:33 PM

ANYTHING ABOUT THIS *NOT* STRIKE YOU AS AN INSIDE JOB?

HMPH.

LOOKS LIKE CAVES DOWN THERE. HAVE YOU CHECKED THEM?

RACHEL WAS BAREFOOT. HOW COULD SHE HAVE CROSSED THE FOREST, CLIMBED THESE ROCKS, AND SCALED THE CLIFF?

NO WAY. IT'D BE IMPOSSIBLE.

SEE THAT MARSHLAND OVER THERE? LIKE A JUNGLE...

A MASS OF BUSHES WITH THORNS THE SIZE OF MY DICK.

TINY, HUH?

4:45 PM

FORT WALTON?

THAT'S RIGHT, ALSO KNOWN AS WARD C.

MORE SEWAGE PROCESSING?

HMPH.

SEWAGE PROCESSING IT IS.

6:37 PM

A LOCKED ROOM. SEVERAL CHECKPOINTS.

THEN A ROOMFUL OF ORDERLIES.

SHE HOPS A WALL WITH AN ELECTRIC SECURITY WIRE, OR A LOCKED GATE.

ALL BAREFOOT.

DIDN'T SEE A GRAVEYARD. PEOPLE MUST DIE AROUND HERE. WHAT DO THEY DO WITH THE BODIES?

HMM. WE'LL HAVE TO CHECK IT OUT.

MEANWHILE LET'S START QUESTIONING THE STAFF. THEY'RE SO HELPFUL.

OKAY, SO LET'S GO OVER WHAT WE'VE LEARNED TONIGHT -- IT SEEMS IMPOSSIBLE FOR RACHEL TO HAVE LEFT HER ROOM, PASSED SEVERAL CHECKPOINTS, AND CROSSED THE AREA WHERE YOU WERE PLAYING CARDS -- ALL WITHOUT BEING SEEN.

UNLESS... SHE HAD HELP. DO WE AGREE, DR. CAWLEY?

A REASONABLE SUPPOSITION.

7:34 PM

THE ISLAND'S BEEN SEARCHED TOP TO BOTTOM -- NOTHING. IT'S EQUALLY UNLIKELY SHE SWAM AWAY, GIVEN THE WATER TEMPERATURE AND STRONG CURRENTS.

MISS MARINO, DID ANYTHING UNUSUAL HAPPEN IN THERAPY LAST NIGHT?

NOTHING, BESIDES THE FACT THAT WE'RE IN A MENTAL HOSPITAL. "USUAL" ISN'T PART OF OUR ROUTINE.

BUT AS FOR THE CONCERNS YOU'VE RAISED...

IN THE INTERESTS OF COOPERATING, WE'RE WAIVING CONFIDENTIALITY. YOU CAN TELL US WHAT WAS SAID.

WE DISCUSSED ANGER MANAGEMENT. A FEW WEEKS AGO, THE NUMBER OF LITTLE TIFFS AND QUARRELS BEGAN TO RISE. SO WE WENT OVER VARIOUS APPROPRIATE, OR INAPPROPRIATE, WAYS OF EXPRESSING ANXIETY.

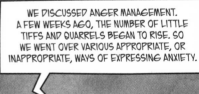

DID RACHEL SOLANDO HAVE ANY RECENT ANGER ISSUES?

NO. THE RAIN MADE HER NERVOUS, BUT THAT'S ALL SHE SAID LAST NIGHT.

DR. SHEEHAN LED THE SESSION. IS HE HERE?

DR. SHEEHAN TOOK THE FERRY THIS MORNING. HE'D ALREADY SCHEDULED A VACATION.

A PATIENT ESCAPES AND YOU LET SOMEONE LEAVE?

HE'S A DOCTOR.

I CAN'T BELIEVE THIS... I NEED HIS PHONE NUMBER.

I REALLY DON'T--

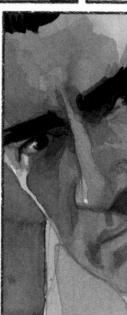

YOU'LL HAVE IT, MARSHAL, YOU'LL HAVE IT.

SORRY, SIR. ALL RADIO COMMUNICATIONS ARE DOWN.

BUT WHY? THE STORM'S NOT THAT BAD YET.

NOT HERE, BUT OVER THERE...

MAYBE IT'LL BLOW OVER BY TOMORROW.

YOU'RE JOKING. IT HASN'T EVEN STARTED YET.

WHAT WILL THE FIELD OFFICE DO IF YOU DON'T CHECK IN?

THEY'LL MARK IT IN THE NIGHTLY REPORT AND START WORRYING AFTER 24 HOURS.

WELL, I'M GOING HOME. IF YOU'D LIKE, COME BY AT NINE AND WE CAN TALK MORE OVER A DRINK.

EXCELLENT! WHAT WONDERFUL DEFENSE MECHANISMS! YOU MUST BE A FORMIDABLE INTERROGATOR.

I'M A FEDERAL MARSHAL. I APPREHEND SUSPECTS. I RARELY QUESTION THEM.

MEN OF VIOLENCE FASCINATE ME.

HELL OF AN ASSUMPTION, DOC.

I CALLED YOU MEN OF VIOLENCE, NOT VIOLENT MEN.

ENLIGHTEN US.

I'LL WAGER THAT SINCE GRADE SCHOOL NEITHER OF YOU HAVE BACKED DOWN FROM A FIGHT. RETREAT IS NOT AN OPTION. AM I RIGHT?

WASN'T RAISED TO RUN.

DO YOU BELIEVE IN GOD?

HAVE YOU EVER SEEN A CONCENTRATION CAMP?

NO.

YOUR ENGLISH IS ALMOST PERFECT. HIT THE CONSONANTS A BIT HARD, MAYBE.

LEGAL IMMIGRATION ISN'T A CRIME, MARSHAL.

BACK TO GOD-- YOU SEE A PLACE LIKE THAT SOMEDAY AND THEN WE'LL TALK AGAIN.

ONCE MORE, YOUR DEFENSE MECHANISMS ARE ASTONISHING.

WHAT ASTONISHES ME IS THE FACT THAT YOUR FACILITY SUFFERED NINE SECURITY BREACHES, AND NO ONE SEEMS INCLINED TO LOOK INTO IT.

DR. NAEHRING ACTS AS LIAISON TO OUR BOARD OF OVERSEERS. I INVITED HIM TONIGHT IN THAT CAPACITY, SO HE COULD ADDRESS YOUR REQUEST.

WHAT REQUEST?

WE WILL NOT RELEASE PERSONNEL FILES OR OUR MEDICAL RECORDS. CONTINUE YOUR INVESTIGATION AND WE'LL HELP AS BEST WE CAN.

NO. THIS INVESTIGATION'S OVER. WE'LL MAKE OUR REPORT. HOOVER'S BOYS CAN PICK IT UP FROM HERE. WE'RE LEAVING.

AS YOU WISH, MARSHAL.

10:37 PM

I WIN AGAIN.

11:47 PM

WE REALLY PACKING IT IN, BOSS?

CAN'T SLEEP?

THEY'RE LYING TO US ABOUT EVERYTHING, AND EVERYONE SEEMS TO BE IN ON IT.

MAYBE MY THREAT'LL WORK, AND TOMORROW CAWLEY WILL RECONSIDER HIS POSITION.

SO YOU *WERE* BLUFFING.

WHEN YOU'VE GOT A HAND YOU PURSE YOUR LIPS. JUST A SECOND, BUT YOU DO IT EVERY TIME.

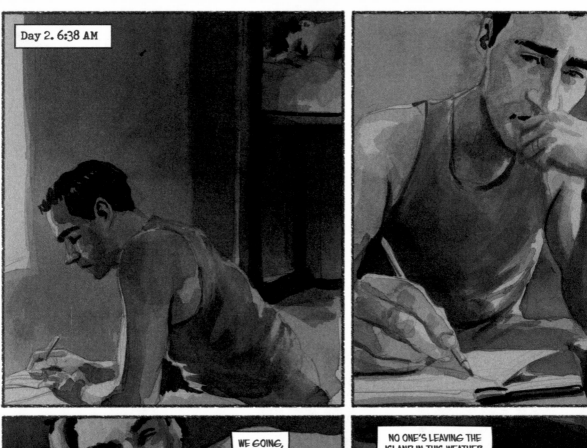

Day 2. 6:38 AM

WE GOING, BOSS?

NO ONE'S LEAVING THE ISLAND IN THIS WEATHER.

The Law of 4
I am 4
They were 80
+ You are 3
We are 4
But
Who is 67?

I SLEPT ON IT, CHUCK. I CRACKED RACHEL'S CODE.

THE TRICK, DOCTOR, IS TO ACTUALLY SLEEP WHEN YOU GO TO BED.

OH, IS THAT IT? I KNEW I FORGOT SOMETHING.

HOW'S DR. NAEHRING THIS MORNING?

I'M SORRY. JEREMIAH IS A GENIUS, BUT RIGHT NOW HE'S OBSESSED WITH HIS NEW BOOK ABOUT MALE WARRIOR CULTURE THROUGH THE AGES.

THE WORLD OF PSYCHIATRY IS AT WAR THESE DAYS, YOU KNOW.

AN IDEOLOGICAL, PHILOSOPHICAL, AND EVEN PSYCHOLOGICAL WAR -- THE OLD SCHOOL BELIEVES IN ELECTROSHOCK THERAPY AND PARTIAL LOBOTOMIES, AND THE NEW PREFERS PSYCHOPHARMACOLOGY. A NEW DRUG, *LITHIUM*, HAS JUST BEEN APPROVED.

IT HELPS RELAX PSYCHOTIC PATIENTS, TAMES THEM. SOON CHAINS WILL BE A THING OF THE PAST. BUT IT TAKES MONEY.

WHAT SCHOOL DO YOU BELONG TO?

I AM A FERVENT BELIEVER IN TALK THERAPY. TREAT A PATIENT WITH RESPECT, LISTEN TO HIM, AND YOU HAVE A SHOT AT COMMUNICATION.

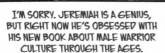

8:22 AM

SO. LOOK AT THIS MESSAGE AGAIN.

IT'S STILL NONSENSE TO ME, MARSHAL.

THE PLUS SIGN PUT ME ON THE RIGHT TRACK.

The Law of 4

I am 47
They were 80

+ You are 3

You are 4

THE DASH UNDER "THEY WERE 80" MEANS YOU HAVE TO ADD THE FIRST TWO LINES.

47+80 EQUALS 127. 1, 2, AND 7.

"PLUS, YOU ARE 3." 1+2+7+3=13. DOES 13 HAVE ANY PARTICULAR IMPORTANCE FOR RACHEL SOLANDO?

IT'S OFTEN SIGNIFICANT FOR SCHIZOPHRENICS.

13, OR 1+3. "WE ARE 4."

SAME THING FOR THE LAST NUMBER. 6+7=13.

IT'S NOT THE LAW OF 4, BUT THE LAW OF 13. THE NAME RACHEL SOLANDO HAS 13 LETTERS IN IT.

IT'S A SIMPLE SUBSTITUTION CODE WHERE A NUMBER STANDS FOR A LETTER.

1 FOR A, 2 FOR B, ETC. YOU SEE?

YES, I THINK SO.

R FOR RACHEL IS 18. A IS 1. ADD THE LETTERS OF HER FIRST NAME: 18+1+3+8+5=12.

47.

THUS "I AM 47." HER FIRST NAME. IF YOU DO THE SAME WITH SOLANDO -- HER SURNAME -- YOU GET 80.

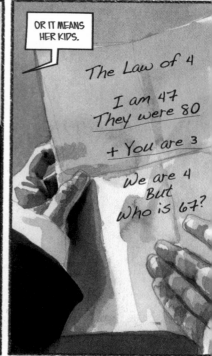

IF WE ADD RACHEL AND 3, WE GET THE NEXT LINE, "WE ARE 4." SO WHO IS 67?

DON'T YOU GET 67 FROM PLAYING WITH THESE NUMBERS?

NO. I THINK IT REFERS TO SOMETHING ON THE ISLAND... DOCTOR?

I CAN'T DECIPHER ALL THIS. I'M TIRED, MARSHAL, VERY TIRED.

I THINK THIS IS A KEY THAT WILL HELP US BREAK FUTURE CODES. SHE'S NOT TRYING TO ESCAPE.

SHE BROUGHT CHUCK AND ME TO THIS ISLAND. THERE MUST BE OTHER CLUES.

RACHEL *BROUGHT* YOU HERE? WHAT FOR?

YOU TELL ME.

I'VE GOT A LONG DAY AHEAD. THERE'S NO FERRY TODAY, SO IF YOU WISH TO PURSUE YOUR INVESTIGATION, I MADE ARRANGEMENTS FOR YOU TO SEE THE PATIENTS WHO WERE AT THE THERAPY SESSION THAT NIGHT.

CAN YOU GIVE US DR. SHEEHAN'S FILE?

NO. AND FOR NOW, WE STILL CAN'T REACH THE MAINLAND.

I'M SCARED OF PENCILS. THEY GO SCRITCH SCRITCH ON PAPER.

2:12 PM

ME?

NO, HIM. HE LOOKS MEAN. LIKE MY DAD AND MY BROTHER.

THEY HIT ME ALL THE TIME.

NOW... I'M SCARED OF YOU.

PETER BREENE	3/20/1930	MALE
The patient attacked his father's nurse with a shard of glass.		
Victim critically injured, scarred for life.		
Patient in denial. Refuses to assume responsibility for his act.		

CAN YOU TELL US ABOUT THE GROUP THERAPY SESSION TWO NIGHTS AGO?

2:25 PM

MY FEET ARE COLD.

WE'LL GIVE YOU SOME SOCKS. WAS RACHEL THERE, AS USUAL?

MY FEET ARE SO COLD!

2:32 PM

I HAVE DARK THOUGHTS. EVERY-ONE DOES...

...BUT NOT EVERYONE KILLS THEIR HUSBAND WITH AN AX.

I'LL NEVER GET OUT. WHAT WOULD I DO OUT THERE ANYWAY?

CAN YOU TELL US ABOUT RACHEL?

SHE WAS NICE. KEPT TO HERSELF. TALKED ABOUT THE RAIN A LOT.

SHE THOUGHT HER KIDS WERE STILL ALIVE, AND SHE WAS STILL AT HOME WITH THEM.

AND WE WERE ALL MAILMEN, MILKMEN, OR DELIVERYMEN STOPPING BY.

~~Peter Breene~~
~~Leonora Grant~~
~~Arthur Toomey~~
Bridget Kearns
She's lying

HMM. HOW WAS DR. SHEEHAN THAT NIGHT?

DR. SHEEHAN'S A GOOD DOCTOR. KIND... HANDSOME.

CAN I GET A GLASS OF WATER, PLEASE?

SURE THING, MRS. KEARNS.

THANK YOU. CAN I GO NOW? I'M TIRED.

SURE. JUST ONE MORE QUESTION. DO YOU KNOW A PATIENT NAMED LAEDDIS?

NO. NEVER HEARD OF HIM.

THINK SHE WAS COACHED?

SHE USED THE EXACT SAME WORDS ABOUT RACHEL AS CAWLEY.

2:55 PM

YOU ASKED ALL THE PATIENTS IF THEY KNEW ANDREW LAEDDIS. WHO'S HE?

WHAT'S THE MATTER? DON'T TRUST ME?

NO. BUT I BROKE THE RULES HERE. I ASKED FOR THIS CASE AS SOON AS IT CAME IN.

WHY?

ANDREW LAEDDIS WAS THE SUPER OF THE BUILDING WHERE MY WIFE AND I LIVED. HE STARTED THE FIRE THAT KILLED HER.

AH, SHIT. SORRY.

YOU WON'T LEAVE HERE. IT'S YOUR PAST AND YOUR FUTURE, TOO.

ROUND AND ROUND IT GOES, LIKE THE MOON AROUND THE EARTH.

THEY'VE GOT SECRETS! THIS HELLHOLE FEEDS ON SECRETS.

C'MON, SETTLE DOWN.

JUST THE KIND OF GIRL YOU BRING HOME TO MOM.

EXCEPT AFTER, SHE BUMPS MOM OFF AND HIDES THE BODY IN THE WOODSHED.

SO... LAEDDIS?

THE SUPER. THEY'D JUST FIRED HIM BEFORE THE ARSON. HE WAS CHARGED BUT NOT CONVICTED. HE HAD A SO-CALLED ALIBI.

ONE DAY, A YEAR LATER, I OPEN UP THE PAPER AND THERE HE IS. THERE WAS A FIRE AT THE SCHOOL WHERE HE WORKED -- HE'D JUST BEEN FIRED. SAME M.O., OVERHEATING BOILER.

HE WAS TRIED AND SAID HE HEARD VOICES. THEY COMMITTED HIM TO SHATTUCK. SOMETHING HAPPENED THERE, AND HE GOT TRANSFERRED HERE SIX MONTHS AGO.

BUT NO ONE'S SEEN HIM.

NOT IN WARDS A OR B. BUT IN C...

YEAH, OR THE GRAVEYARD.

MAYBE. ONE MORE REASON TO CHECK.

WHAT IF HE'S NOT DEAD WHEN YOU FIND HIM? WHAT WILL YOU DO?

I DON'T KNOW.

C'MON, BOSS, DON'T BULLSHIT ME.

ALL I KNOW IS DOLORES DIED IN THE FIRE, AND HE WAS RESPONSIBLE.

WHATEVER HAPPENS, I GOT YOU COVERED. BUT WE NEED TO BE STRAIGHT. I NEED TO KNOW WHAT TO EXPECT FROM NOW ON. I GET THE FEELING YOU'RE HERE TO DO SOME DAMAGE.

I DON'T WANT TO KILL HIM.

I'M NOT SURE I BUY THAT. IF IT WAS MY WIFE -- I'D MURDER HIM.

I HAD ENOUGH KILLING IN THE WAR. I KILLED SO MANY MEN I LOST COUNT.

THE CASE IS THE IMPORTANT THING. I'M REALLY HERE FOR RACHEL SOLANDO.

OKAY, WE'RE OUT NOW. LET'S LOOK AT THE GRAVEYARD. MAYBE THERE'S A LAEDDIS HEADSTONE, AND THAT'LL BE THAT.

ALL RIGHT.

WHAT DID THAT WOMAN WRITE IN YOUR NOTEBOOK?

YOU DON'T MISS A TRICK.

RUN

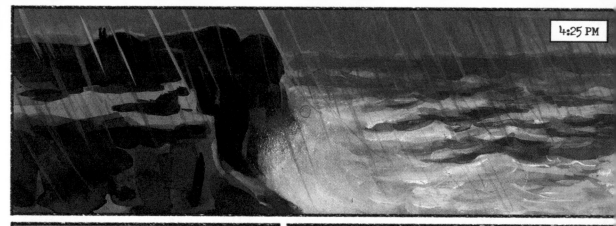

4:25 PM

WHAT'RE THOSE? ROCK PILES? HOW MANY DO YOU COUNT?

FROM HERE... ELEVEN.

ME TOO. LET'S GO DOWN. I WANT TO CHECK.

WE MISCOUNTED. LOOK. ONE THERE, AND ONE OVER THERE, TOO.

THAT MAKES 13. ANOTHER CODE?

MAYBE.

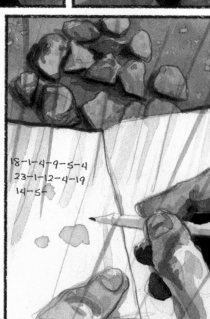

18-1-4-9-5-4
23-1-12-4-19
14-5-

SO TELL ME WHAT YOU KNOW ABOUT THIS PLACE, BOSS.

RUMOR HAS IT IT'S A FACILITY WHERE THEY EXPERIMENT ON THE MIND.

EVER HEARD OF PHENCYCLIDINE? LSD OR MESCALINE?

NO.

HALLUCINOGENS. DRUGS THAT MAKE YOU SEE THINGS. IN LARGE QUANTITIES, THEY CAN APPARENTLY PRODUCE EFFECTS NEARLY IDENTICAL TO ACUTE SCHIZOPHRENIA.

NOW WHAT DO YOU THINK HAPPENS IF YOU GIVE ACUTE SCHIZOPHRENICS HALLUCINOGENS?

THEY WOULDN'T DO THAT TO PEOPLE.

WELL, ANIMALS DON'T GET SCHIZOPHRENIA. NOT YET, ANYWAY. SO TO ABLE TO TEST--

THEY GIVE IT TO HUMAN BEINGS?

BINGO. THEY TOLD ME TO GATHER INFORMATION ON THEIR ACTIVITIES.

WHO'S "THEY"?

IT ALL STARTED WITH LAEDDIS. A YEAR AGO I MADE UP A STORY SO I COULD GO QUESTION HIM AT SHATTUCK. HE WASN'T THERE. HE'D BEEN TRANSFERRED TO *ASHECLIFFE.* SO I ASKED AROUND ABOUT ASHECLIFFE AT OTHER MENTAL HOSPITALS.

EVERYONE HAD HEARD OF IT BUT NO ONE WANTED TO TALK ABOUT IT. ONE HOSPITAL DIRECTOR TOLD ME IT WAS CLASSIFIED.

SO YOU CAME AS SOON AS YOU COULD.

I GOT LUCKY. AN ESCAPED PATIENT. THEY OFFERED ME THE CASE AND TOLD ME TO PICK A PARTNER.

LUCK... YOU THINK YOU REALLY LANDED THIS CASE BY *LUCK?*

YOU'D BEEN ASKING AROUND ABOUT ASHECLIFFE. THEY HAD THEIR EYE ON YOU. WHAT IF THEY LURED US HERE?

HOW COULD THEY KNOW I'D GET THE SOLANDO CASE?

DON'T BE NAÏVE, BOSS. YOU SAID THEY TOLD YOU TO GATHER INFORMATION.

WHO ARE "THEY"?

THE OPERATION SHOULD'VE CALMED HIM DOWN. HOW'D HE WIND UP IN A FIGHT?

APPARENTLY IT DIDN'T WORK.

MARSHALS! IF YOU'RE OUT HERE, PLEASE SIGNAL!

THEY FOUND US. HOW ABOUT THAT.

IT'S AN ISLAND, BOSS.

5:58 PM

WE'RE IN THE MIDDLE OF A *HURRICANE* AND YOU GO FOR A *STROLL?!* WINDS ARE SUPPOSED TO HIT 150 MPH TONIGHT.

MCPHERSON, HOW DO YOU KNOW THAT IF COMMUNICATIONS ARE CUT OFF?

HAM RADIO.

DR. CAWLEY WANTS TO SEE YOU. TAKE A SHOWER AND WE'LL GIVE YOU SOME DRY CLOTHES.

DEAR COLLEAGUES, MAY I PRESENT THE MARSHALS I'VE MENTIONED, DANIELS AND AULE.

DELIGHTED TO SEE YOU, GENTLEMEN.

GENTLEMEN, I HEAR THEY FOUND YOU IN A MAUSOLEUM?

I'D RECOMMEND IT AS A PORT IN A STORM.

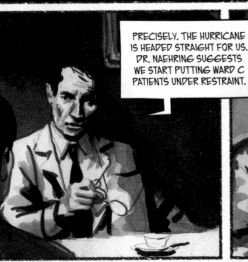

PRECISELY. THE HURRICANE IS HEADED STRAIGHT FOR US. DR. NAEHRING SUGGESTS WE START PUTTING WARD C PATIENTS UNDER RESTRAINT.

WE CAN'T DO THAT. IF IT FLOODS, THEY'LL ALL DROWN.

THAT'D TAKE QUITE A LOT OF FLOODING.

WE VERY WELL MAY GET "A LOT OF FLOODING." DOUBLE THE NUMBER OF GUARDS IN WARD C.

IF THERE'S A BLACKOUT, ALL THE CELLS WILL OPEN.

EXCEPT THERE AREN'T. COUNT AND COUNT AGAIN, YOU WON'T FIND MORE THAN 66. YOUR THEORY DOESN'T HOLD WATER -- UNDERSTAND?

NO, I DON'T. WHAT'S MORE, MY PARTNER AND I WOULD LIKE TO SEE THE PATIENTS' RECORDS.

IMPOSSIBLE.

WE DON'T HAVE ACCESS TO ANYTHING. HOW DO YOU EXPECT US TO FIND HER?

DIDN'T THE WARDEN TELL YOU?

THE WARDEN?

WE STILL HAVEN'T MET HIM.

WE FOUND HER THIS AFTERNOON.

SHE'S IN A ROOM AT THE END OF THE HALLWAY.

GENTLEMEN, YOUR SEARCH IS OVER.

7:04 PM

RACHEL? WE BROUGHT SOME FRIENDS.

I HOPE YOU DIDN'T COME TO SELL ME ANYTHING. I DON'T WANT TO BE RUDE, BUT MY HUSBAND MAKES ALL THE DECISIONS.

NO, WE'VE COME FOR SOMETHING ELSE.

I'M LISTENING.

CAN YOU TELL ME WHERE YOU SPENT THE DAY YESTERDAY?

HERE, AT HOME. WHO ARE THOSE MEN?

POLICE OFFICERS.

WAS JIM IN AN ACCIDENT?

NO, HE'S FINE.

IS IT THE CHILDREN? THEY WENT TO PLAY IN THE YARD. DID THEY DO SOMETHING STUPID?

NO. ACTUALLY, WE'RE INVESTIGATING SOMEONE. WE KEEP GETTING DIFFERENT INFORMATION. MAYBE YOU'VE SEEN HIM. CAN YOU TELL ME ABOUT YOUR DAY YESTERDAY?

WELL... I MADE BREAKFAST FOR JIM AND THE KIDS. JIM LEFT AND THE KIDS WENT TO SCHOOL. I DECIDED TO GO FOR A SWIM IN THE LAKE.

DO YOU GO OFTEN?

NO. I WAS JUST... OUT OF SORTS.

I TOOK OFF MY CLOTHES AND SWAM UNTIL MY ARMS AND LEGS FELT LIKE LOGS. THEN I GOT OUT AND MADE SAND CASTLES.

HOW MANY? DO YOU RECALL?

YES. 13.

THAT'S A LOT.

AND AFTER THAT?

I THOUGHT ABOUT YOU.

BECAUSE YOU'RE MY JIM.

SIT DOWN.

I MISSED YOU. YOU'RE NEVER HERE.

WE SHOULD SEIZE THE DAY, TAKE LIFE AS IT COMES.

WHAT DID YOU DO AFTER THE SAND CASTLES?

YOU KNOW QUITE WELL. DON'T YOU REMEMBER, OR DO YOU WANT TO HEAR ME SAY IT?

I WANT TO HEAR YOU SAY IT.

I CAME HOME ALL WET... AND YOU LICKED ME DRY.

UM... WHAT ELSE DID YOU DO YESTERDAY?

I BURIED YOU.

HERE I AM.

I BURIED YOU IN AN EMPTY COFFIN BECAUSE YOUR BODY EXPLODED OVER THE NORTH ATLANTIC.

YOUR BODY BURNED UP AND GOT EATEN BY SHARKS.

THEY... THEY KILLED MY JIM. WHO ARE YOU, DAMMIT?

WHO IS THAT *BASTARD?* YOU WANTED TO FUCK ME, HUH? *RAPIST!* JIM'LL SLIT YOUR THROAT!

WHERE ARE MY BABIES?! *MY BABIES!* GIVE THEM BACK!

WE'LL COME BACK AND SEE YOU A BIT LATER, RACHEL.

7:32 PM

WHERE'D YOU FIND HER?

ON THE BEACH, BY THE LIGHTHOUSE.

YOU'RE DEATHLY PALE, MARSHAL. ARE YOU ALL RIGHT?

YOU OKAY, BOSS?

IT'S JUST... A MIGRAINE.

DO YOU GET THEM OFTEN?

SIX OR SEVEN TIMES A YEAR.

HERE, TAKE THESE. THEY'LL KNOCK YOU OUT AN HOUR OR TWO, BUT THEN YOU'LL BE GOOD AS NEW.

I'M OKAY, THANKS.

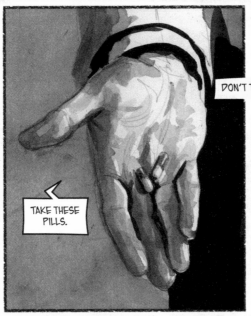

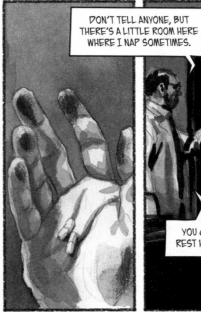

SHE'S HERE. SHE'S GOING TO CATCH US.

LAEDDIS?

NO GRUDGES, PAL?

AAAHH

HELP ME. I'LL BECOME DOLORES.

RACHEL.

I'LL BE YOUR WIFE.

SHE'LL COME BACK TO YOU.

I'M NOT YOUR DAD. IT'S NOT MY JOB.

THEN I'LL CALL YOU DAD.

WHY ARE YOU A BAD SAILOR?

I DON'T LIKE WATER

GIVE THEM BACK.

IF YOU LOVE ME, GIVE THEM BACK.

I THINK THAT'S WHY I STOPPED DRINKING.

AT LEAST YOU'RE NOT DELUDING YOURSELF.

PERHAPS I COULD RECOMMEND SOME COLLEAGUES OF MINE. PSYCHOANALYSTS.

MARSHALS DON'T SEE SHRINKS. I'D GET PENSIONED OUT.

AS YOU WISH. BUT THE PROBLEM'S NOT GOING AWAY.

YOU DON'T KNOW A THING.

DON'T KID YOURSELF. I SPECIALIZE IN *GRIEF TRAUMA* AND *SURVIVOR'S GUILT*. YOU SURVIVED THE WAR, AND YOU MUST HAVE SUFFERED TERRIBLE GRIEF AFTER YOUR WIFE'S DEATH.

I...DON'T KNOW.

11:47 PM

YOU ALL RIGHT? HAD ME SCARED THERE.

AT FIRST I THOUGHT YOU WERE FAKING TO GET TO THE PERSONNEL FILES.

I'M NOT THAT SNEAKY.

GAVE ME AN IDEA, ANYWAY.

YOU DIDN'T--

YEP. HE LEFT HIS OFFICE FOR A MINUTE. I WAS OFFICIALLY WATCHING OVER YOU. BUT I DIDN'T FIND ANYTHING.

THE FILING CABINETS WERE LOCKED. BUT I CHECKED HIS DESK AND HIS CALENDAR.

YESTERDAY, TODAY, TOMORROW, AND THE DAY AFTER WERE ALL BLOCKED OUT.

MARKED OFF IN BLACK.

THE HURRICANE.

HE WROTE SOMETHING ACROSS THOSE DAYS... *PATIENT 67.*

2:42 PM

--JUST CAN'T CRANK OUT THE VOLTAGE, DR. CAWLEY, AND WE'VE GOT THOSE TWO PATIENTS IN CRITICAL.

I'LL BE THERE SOON.

AUXILIARY GENERATOR'S DOWN. DON'T SEE ANY LIGHTS AT ALL.

SO THE FENCES ARE DOWN, TOO.

LET'S SEE.

LOOKS LIKE IT.

THAT MEANS THE FRONT GATES AND THE CELLS AS WELL. LET'S VISIT THE FORT.

THE MISSING PATIENT WAS FOUND. YOU DON'T HAVE AUTHORIZATION.

LISTEN, SHIT HEEL, WE'RE FEDERAL MARSHALS ON A FEDERAL FACILITY. I CAN SHOOT YOU IN THE BALLS, AND NO COURT WOULD LIFT A FINGER. SO OPEN THAT GATE.

I SAID OPEN--

OKAY.

EXCUSE ME? I DIDN'T HEAR YOU.

YES, SIR. UNDERSTOOD.

HEY, DIDN'T KNOW YOU WERE SUCH A BALLBREAKER. ARMY MUST'VE LOVED YOU.

GOT A GOLD MEDAL IN GIVING PEOPLE SHIT.

SERIOUSLY... LAEDDIS IS HERE. I CRACKED RACHEL'S ROCKPILE CODE. IT WAS HIS NAME--ANDREW LAEDDIS.

PATIENT 67, YOU THINK?

I DO INDEED.

WE'RE SCREWED.

UNLESS WE FIND A WATER DUCT OR SOMETHING.

WE'RE JUST GOING TO WALK RIGHT IN. WE'RE NOT DRESSED LIKE MARSHALS. NO ONE'LL NOTICE. THEY'RE TOO BUSY.

AMEN.

HEY.

THEY SENT US TO LEND THE CLEANING CREW A HAND.

GO ON. THERE'S A LOT OF DAMAGE, ESPECIALLY 'ROUND BACK.

I'M NOT COMPLAINING, BUT THAT WAS TOO EASY.

WE JUST GOT LUCKY. I'LL TRY NOT TO PURSE MY LIPS THIS TIME.

BETTER SQUEEZE YOUR BUTT CHEEKS INSTEAD.

NINETY-EIGHT BOTTLES OF BEER ON THE WALL...

YOU CAN'T DO THAT DAMMIT! YOU CAN'T!

FIRST TIME, HUH? YOU GET USED TO IT. YOU GET USED TO EVERYTHING.

THEY SENT US HERE TO LEND A HAND OUT BACK.

UPSTAIRS, CROSS AND TURN RIGHT. WE GOT ALL THE LOONIES LOCKED UP NOW, 'CEPT A FEW.

BILLINGS, CALM DOWN! NOWHERE TO RUN, HEAR?

TAG!

YOU WIN.

YOU'RE RIGHT, CHUCK. LET'S GET OUT.

HELP! HURRY, DAMMIT!

THE FILES MUST BE HERE SOMEWHERE. YOU LOOK FOR LAEDDIS, I'LL FIND THE FILES.

BOSS, I THINK THE FARTHER DOWN YOU GO, THE WORSE IT GETS. THE OFFICE HAS GOT TO BE UP TOP.

OKAY. MEET YOU IN 15 MINUTES IN THE BIG HALL.

WATCH YOUR ASS.

C'MON CHAMP. TIME FOR YOUR MASSAGE. DON'T WANT MY STAR DROPPING ON ME FROM A CRAMP.

NO. HOW COULD I...?

AFTER ALL YOUR PRETTY WORDS, HERE I AM, BACK IN THIS HELLHOLE, THANKS TO YOU.

HOW DID THEY GET YOU? YOU CAN'T JUST WALK INTO A PRISON AND TAKE WHOEVER YOU WANT. THERE HAVE TO BE EVALS. PAPERWORK.

HA HA!

YOU KNOW WHAT CAWLEY SPECIALIZES IN?

YEAH. SURVIVOR'S GUILT.

OOOOH, NO. VIOLENCE.

ESPECIALLY IN MALES.

NO, NAEHRING'S THE--

SCRATCH

CAWLEY! HE MAKES SURE HE GETS ALL THE MOST VIOLENT CRIMINALS AND FELONS. WHY DO YOU THINK HE HAS SO FEW PATIENTS?

HOW DID THEY GET TO YOU?

I'M SURE YOU'VE WORKED WITH HIM BEFORE.

I KNOW THE GUY. I TRUST HIM.

DO YOU? YOU DIDN'T SMOKE ANY OF HIS CIGARETTES, DID YOU?

THEY'VE WON.

YOU CAN'T KILL LAEDDIS AND ALSO EXPOSE THE TRUTH. YOU HAVE TO CHOOSE. DO YOU HEAR ME?

WHERE IS HE?

SHE'S DEAD. LET HER GO.

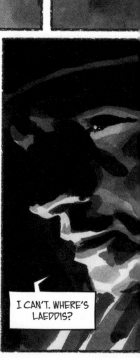

I CAN'T. WHERE'S LAEDDIS?

SCRATCH

THOUGHT WE WERE MEETING IN THE BIG HALL.

CAWLEY AND THE WARDEN ARE HERE. I WAS COMING OUT OF THE RECORDS ROOM WHEN I SAW THEM. I DON'T THINK THEY SAW ME, BUT WE BETTER GO.

POWER'S BACK. THAT'S NOT GOING TO MAKE IT ANY EASIER.

SURE. PLEASE HOLD.

HEY YOU! WAIT A MINUTE!

STOP! I NEED TO TALK TO YOU!

4:17 PM

OH MAN, I THOUGHT OUR GOOSE WAS COOKED.

WE HAVE TO ASSUME THEY'LL FIND OUT WE WERE IN THERE.

SO DID YOU FIND LAEDDIS?

I FOUND GEORGE NOYCE.

HE'S HERE, THEN?

THEY ROUGHED HIM UP. HE'S AFRAID TO WIND UP LIKE THE REST, LIKE LAEDDIS... AT THE LIGHTHOUSE.

YOU REALLY THINK THEY'RE DOING HUMAN EXPERIMENTS THERE?

A SEWAGE PLANT SURROUNDED BY A FENCE AND GUARDS? WHAT DO YOU THINK?

IT WAS QUIETER IN SEATTLE.

I KNEW A GUY IN THE OFFICE THERE. NAME OF JOE...

IT'S NOT THE JOES I MISS. LOOK WHAT I FOUND.

JOE FAIRFIELD, HIS NAME WAS.

NEVER HEARD OF HIM. LOOK--THE INTAKE FORM FOR LAEDDIS. NO PHOTO, NOTHING. WEIRD, HUH?

DON'T YOU WANT A LOOK?

LATER. WE'RE GOING.

WHERE?

THE LIGHTHOUSE.

5:02 PM

5:55 PM

I THINK WE'RE LOST.

WOODS THIN OUT OVER THERE.

TO SHOW GOD I'VE LEARNED FROM HIS EXAMPLE.

GOD GIVES US NATURE, THAT SMILING KILLER WITH ITS HURRICANES AND EARTHQUAKES. NO MORAL ORDER IS PURER THAN THIS STORM. THERE IS NO MORAL ORDER AT ALL.

THERE'S ONLY ONE QUESTION--IS YOUR VIOLENCE STRONGER THAN MINE?

I'M NOT VIOLENT.

YOU'RE VIOLENT AS THEY COME... LIKE ME.

WITHOUT SOCIAL CONSTRAINTS, YOU WOULDN'T HESITATE TO CRACK MY SKULL OPEN IF I WERE YOUR ONLY MEAL.

AND IF I BIT YOUR EYE, COULD YOU STOP ME BEFORE I TORE IT OUT?

TRY IT.

NOW YOU'RE GETTING THE IDEA.

HE THINKS IT DOESN'T POSE A THREAT.

WHAT?

YOUR LITTLE GAME. HE THINKS IT'S HARMLESS. NOT ME.

8:32 PM

MARSHAL! WHERE WERE YOU?!

SIGHTSEEING. MEETING OVER?

YES. SOMEONE WAS DISTURBING THE PATIENT IN THE FORT. HE SPENT SOME TIME WITH THE PARANOID SCHIZOPHRENIC GEORGE NOYCE.

OH?

YES. NOYCE SPINS TALL TALES THAT TEND TO AGITATE PEOPLE. TWO WEEKS AGO HE WENT SO FAR THAT A PATIENT ATTACKED HIM.

WHAT KIND OF STORIES?

PARANOID DELUSIONS. THE WORLD IS OUT TO GET HIM. THAT SORT OF THING.

WELL, WITH RACHEL BACK, YOU'LL BE ABLE TO LEAVE SOON. THERE'S A FERRY AT EIGHT.

SURE. JUST WAKE US UP.

US?

YES. YOU HAVEN'T SEEN HIM, HAVE YOU?

WHO?

MY PARTNER, CHUCK.

YOU HAVE NO PARTNER, MARSHAL. YOU CAME ALONE.

TELL ME ABOUT YOUR... PARTNER.

WHAT PARTNER

I WON'T EVEN ASK YOU IF YOU'VE SEEN MY PARTNER. I SUPPOSE HE'S AT THE LIGHTHOUSE, LIKE ALL THE TROUBLEMAKERS.

WHO'RE YOU TALKING ABOUT?

NO ONE. JUST KIDDING.

STORM DID SOME REAL DAMAGE. DID YOU FIX EVERYTHING UP?

ALMOST. BUSTED UP THE ELECTRICAL SYSTEM BAD. WE ONLY GOT TO PART OF IT.

ISN'T THAT DANGEROUS? WON'T THE CRAZIES TRY SOMETHING?

WE AIN'T DUMB. WE'RE NOT GONNA TELL EVERYONE.

STILL A LOT OF WORK TO DO?

THE WHOLE SOUTHWEST CORNER'S STILL DOWN, BUT RIGHT NOW THE PATIENTS ARE ASLEEP. THE WIRES'LL BE WORKING TOMORROW MORNING BY SEVEN.

SO THERE'S A WAY OUT.

Day 4. 3:28 AM

WHY ARE YOUR HANDS SHAKING, SWEETHEART?

WHY DON'T YOU RUN AWAY?

7:01 AM

THIS IS IT, MY LOVE. JUST ME, LAEDDIS, AND CHUCK.

SO YOU STILL TRUST HIM?

POK

BUT HIS HANDS, SWEETIE——THEY DON'T FIT HIM.

DROP YOUR GUN AND TURN AROUND.

IT'S EMPTY. HADN'T YOU NOTICED?

CLAC

PUT IT DOWN AND DRY YOURSELF OF

WHAT'S BEHIND THAT CURTAIN?

WE'LL GET TO THAT. ARE THE GUARDS WOUNDED?

NO.

YES, HE'S HERE. TELL DR. SHEEHAN TO CHECK ON THE GUARDS BEFORE COMING UP.

AH, THE MYSTERIOUS *DR. SHEEHAN.* DID HE COME ON THE FERRY THIS MORNING?

HE NEVER LEFT THE ISLAND.

HE'S A BRILLIANT PSYCHIATRIST. THIS WHOLE THING WAS OUR IDEA.

HOW'D YOU MANAGE IT? GUY AT THE MARSHAL'S OFFICE? NO, WAIT-- HAD THE GUY AT THE NEWSSTAND IN BOSTON SPIKE MY MORNING COFFEE?

NOT BOSTON. HERE. YOU'VE BEEN A *PATIENT* HERE FOR *TWO YEARS.*

WHAT? I'M A FEDERAL MARSHAL.

WERE. DO YOU REMEMBER ANYTHING BEFORE YOU WOKE UP IN THE BATHROOM ON THE FERRY?

RIGHT. YOU CAME HERE TO FIND THIS DOCUMENT FOR SENATOR HURLY.

PROOF THERE'S A 67TH PATIENT WHOSE EXISTENCE WE DENIED, INTENDED TO SHUT US DOWN.

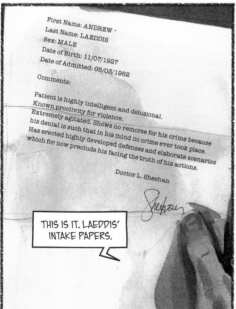

First Name: ANDREW
Last Name: LAEDDIS
Sex: MALE
Date of Birth: 11/07/1927
Date of Admitted: 06/03/1952

Comments:

Patient is highly intelligent and delusional.
Known proclivity for violence.
Extremely agitated. Shows no remorse for his crime because
his denial is such that in his mind no crime ever took place.
Has erected highly developed defenses and elaborate scenarios
which for now preclude his facing the truth of his actions.

Doctor L. Sheehan

THIS IS IT. LAEDDIS' INTAKE PAPERS.

EDWARD DANIELS
ANDREW LAEDDIS

RACHEL SOLANDO
DOLORES CHANAL

THERE'S YOUR LAW OF 4.

WHAT IS THIS?

LOOK CAREFULLY. TELL ME WHAT THESE NAMES HAVE IN COMMON. YOU'RE THE GENIUS CODEBREAKER.

THEY'VE GOT 13 LETTERS. SO?

ES. WHAT ELSE?

13 LETTERS. THAT'S IT. LISTEN--

EDWARD DANIELS
ANDREW ...DIS
RACHEL ...DO
DOL...

THEY'RE THE SAME LETTERS. *ANAGRAMS.*

NO.

WARD DANIELS
DREW LAEDDIS
HEL SOLANDO
LORES CHANAL

"NO," THEY'RE NOT THE SAME, OR "NO," YOU WON'T ADMIT THE TRUTH?

ANDREW LAEDDIS, AN ANAGRAM OF EDWARD DANIELS. RACHEL SOLANDO, AN ANAGRAM OF DOLORES CHANAL. YOU CAME FOR THE TRUTH? THERE IT IS... ANDREW.

TEDDY!

DWARD DANIE
NDRE...
...
OL...

YOUR NAME IS *ANDREW LAEDDIS.* THE *67TH PATIENT* AT ASHECLIFFE IS *YOU,* ANDREW.

ARE YOU FUCKING WITH ME?

YOU WERE COMMITTED HERE 22 MONTHS AGO BY COURT ORDER BECAUSE YOU COMMITTED A CRIME SOCIETY DEEMED UNFORGIVABLE. BUT NOT ME, ANDREW.

MY NAME IS... EDWARD DANIELS.

NO, *ANDREW LAEDDIS.* YOU COULDN'T FORGIVE YOURSELF FOR WHAT YOU DID, SO YOU CREATED A COMPLEX SCENARIO WHERE YOU WERE THE HERO. YOU CONVINCED YOURSELF YOU WERE A MARSHAL WHO'D COME TO INVESTIGATE A CONSPIRACY HERE ON SHUTTER ISLAND.

MAYBE WE *SHOULD* LET YOU LIVE IN YOUR FANTASY WORLD. I'D BE FINE WITH THAT.

BUT YOU'RE VIOLENT. VERY VIOLENT. BECAUSE OF YOUR TRAINING, YOU'RE THE MOST VIOLENT PATIENT WE HAVE HERE AT ASHECLIFFE.

ANDREW, IT'S BEEN DECIDED THAT IF I CAN'T MAKE YOU SEE REASON, PERMANENT MEASURES WILL HAVE TO BE TAKEN. DO YOU UNDERSTAND?

NICE ACT YOU GOT GOING, DOC.

ANDREW. I'M ALL YOU'VE GOT. I'VE BEEN LISTENING TO THE SAME DELUSION FOR 2 YEARS NOW. I KNOW EVERY DETAIL, EVEN YOUR DREAMS. DOLORES SOAKING WET WITH A LEAKING BELLY. THE LOGS--

SHUT UP.

HOW ELSE COULD I KNOW, ANDREW?

YOU DRUGGED ME. THAT FOOD. THOSE CIGARETTES, AND THE PILLS. IT ALL STARTED THEN, AFTER MY MIGRAINE.

WE'RE OUT OF TIME. I HAD 4 DAYS. IF I FAIL, A MORE RADICAL APPROACH WILL BE NECESSARY.

TOO BAD.

ANDREW, RACHEL SOLANDO AND YOUR WIFE HAVE THE SAME LETTERS IN THEIR NAMES AND THEY BOTH KILLED THEIR CHILDREN THE SAME WAY. HOW DO YOU EXPLAIN THAT?

WE NEVER HAD KIDS.

LOOK AT THIS.

EDWARD LAEDDIS
DANIEL LAEDDIS
RACHEL LAEDDIS

YOUR CHILDREN, ANDREW.

RACHEL SOLANDO'S CHILDREN, AND HER HOUSE BY THE LAKE.

YOUR HOUSE. YOU BOUGHT IT FOR YOUR WIFE TO GET HER OUT OF THE CITY. SHE WAS SICK. MANIC DEPRESSIVE AND SUICIDAL.

EDWARD LAEDDIS
DANIEL LAEDDIS
RACHEL LAEDDIS

YOU LIE.

SHE ABUSED THE CHILDREN. SHE WAS A DANGER TO HERSELF––

WE HAD NO CHILDREN. WE TRIED, BUT COULDN'T.

LOOK AT THEM, ANDREW. HAVE YOU SEEN THEM IN YOUR DREAMS RECENTLY? DID THE LITTLE GIRL LEAD YOU TO YOUR GRAVESTONE?

YOU'RE A BAD SAILOR. YOUR FATHER SAILED. IN OTHER WORDS, YOU'RE A BAD FATHER. YOU DIDN'T SAVE THEM.

YOU DRUGGED ME! YOU WANT TO GET RID OF ME AND MY PARTNER BECAUSE I FOUND OUT WHAT YOU'RE UP TO HERE.

REALLY? TELL ME, YOU'VE BEEN ALL OVER THE ISLAND. WHERE ARE THE NAZI DOCTORS?

YOU'RE RUNNING AN EXPERIMENTAL HOSPITAL.

TRUE.

YOU TAKE ONLY THE MOST VIOLENT PATIENTS.

THE MOST VIOLENT AND THE MOST DELUSIONAL.

YOU DO EXPERIMENTS ON THEM!

I PLEAD GUILTY.

SURGICAL EXPERIMENTS.

AH, NO, SORRY. WE OPERATE ONLY AS A LAST RESORT AND *ALWAYS* OVER MY MOST VOCAL PROTESTS. BUT I CAN'T CHANGE PEOPLE'S MINDS ALONE.

LET ME LEAVE THE ISLAND. I'M A FEDERALLY APPOINTED OFFICER OF THE LAW. YOU CAN'T KEEP ME HERE.

YOU WIN, MARSHAL. HERE. IS THIS YOURS?

ARE THOSE YOUR INITIALS ON THE BUTT?

YES.

IS IT LOADED?

I CAN FEEL THE WEIGHT.

THEN SHOOT ME. IT'S THE ONLY WAY YOU'LL LEAVE.

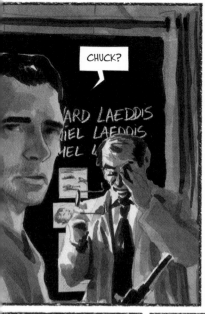

CHUCK?

NO. *DR. LESTER SHEEHAN.* YOU CALLED ME CHUCK AULE--AS IN "CHUCKLE"-- AS A JOKE.

NOW I UNDERSTAND YOUR AWKWARD HANDS... DOCTOR.

YOU WERE SPYING ON ME THIS WHOLE TIME.

JUST MAKING SURE YOU WEREN'T IN ANY DANGER. I'VE BEEN YOUR PRIMARY PSYCHIATRIST FOR TWO YEARS. DON'T YOU RECOGNIZE ME, ANDREW?

MY NAME'S TEDDY.

THIS IS ALL PART OF YOUR PLAY. INCLUDING MY DISAPPEARANCE.

EVEN THE HURRICANE? YOU FAKE THAT, TOO?

NO, BUT YOU CAN PREDICT ONE, ESPECIALLY ON AN ISLAND.

YOU NEVER GIVE UP, DO YOU?

THE STORM WAS ESSENTIAL TO YOUR FANTASY. WE SIMPLY WAITED FOR ONE.

YOUR NOTEBOOK. WANT TO TRY AND CRACK THE LAST CODE?

ANDREW, WE HAVEN'T MUCH TIME LEFT. NAEHRING'S GOT AN *OPERATING ROOM* RESERVED FOR YOU. YOU'RE GOING TO HAVE *SURGERY.*

A LOBOTOMY. LIKE NOYCE. IS THAT IT? UNLESS HE ISN'T REAL EITHER.

GEORGE NOYCE IS QUITE REAL. EVERYTHING YOU TOLD DR. SHEEHAN IS REAL, EXCEPT THAT YOU DIDN'T MEET HIM IN PRISON, BUT IN HERE. HE'S BEEN HERE SINCE 1950.

HE IMPROVED, AND WE TRANSFERRED HIM FROM WARD C TO A. BUT YOU ATTACKED HIM.

WHO?

YOU. TWO WEEKS AGO. YOU ALMOST KILLED HIM BECAUSE HE CALLED YOU LAEDDIS.

NO. I SAW HIM YESTERDAY AND—

I KNOW. I HAVE A TRANSCRIPT OF THE CONVERSATION. SHALL I READ IT?

"NO, IT WAS ALL ABOUT YOU. ABOUT LAEDDIS. I'M JUST A MEANS TO AN END FOR YOU."

NO. THAT'S—

WHEN YOU ASKED HIM WHO HAD HURT HIM, HE SAID—-YOU.

BECAUSE IT WAS MY FAULT, NOT BECAUSE I DID IT.

"THIS IS A GAME, GET IT? AN INCREDIBLE SETUP. ALL THIS IS FOR YOU."

HE'S CRAZY, HE... WHAT ABOUT THE OTHERS? NO ONE SAID A THING.

THEY'RE USED TO IT AND YOU FRIGHTEN THEM. YOU'VE BEEN STICKING YOUR PLASTIC BADGE INTO THEIR FACES FOR TWO YEARS.

25-1-18-20-
13-8-9-15-5
Y-A-R-U-M-
H-I-O-E

YOU ARE HIM

IT'S OUR LAST CHANCE, ANDREW. ADMIT WHAT YOU'VE DONE. OPEN YOUR EYES, OR WE WON'T BE ABLE TO HELP.

MY NAME'S TEDDY, NOT ANDREW.

2:17 PM

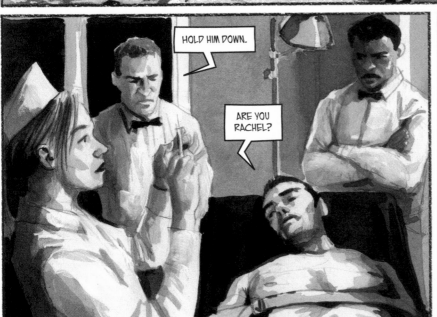

HOLD HIM DOWN.

ARE YOU RACHEL?

YOUR HAIR WAS DYED BLACK? SO THOSE WERE THE MARKS ON MY FINGERS.

YOU'RE AN EXCELLENT ACTRESS. I REALLY THOUGHT YOU WERE CRAZY.

MY NAME'S EMILY.

NO, NO, NO,
NOOOO--

LET'S PUT THEM IN THE KITCHEN. THEY'LL BE OUR DOLLS.

BE QUIET.

WE'LL GO PICNIC TOMORROW.

BE QUIET, DOLORES... PLEASE BE QUIET.

HELP ME. *FREE ME.*

WE'LL GIVE THEM BATHS.

DOLORES...

I LOVE YOU.

I LOVE YOU, TOO.

BANG

DOLORES!

DOLORES WHO?

DOLORES LAEDDIS.

WHO'S SHE?

MY WIFE. I KILLED HER BECAUSE SHE KILLED OUR THREE KIDS.

WE REACHED THIS BREAKTHROUGH BEFORE, A FEW MONTHS AGO. BUT YOU HAD A REGRESSION. WE CAN'T RISK THAT AGAIN.

IT WON'T HAPPEN AGAIN. MY NAME IS *ANDREW LAEDDIS*. I'M HERE BECAUSE I CAN'T FACE THE FACT THAT I KILLED MY OWN WIFE.

Day 5. 9:26 AM